D1096311

Merry Christmas Kimberly
Love, Charles
1974

SUNFLOWERS FOR TINA

SUNFLOWERS

FOR TINA

ANNE NORRIS BALDWIN

illustrated by ANN GRIFALCONI

FOUR WINDS PRESS • NEW YORK

by the same author
THE SOMETIMES ISLAND

Second Printing, 1972
First Printing, 1970

Published by Four Winds Press
A Division of Scholastic Magazines, Inc., New York, N.Y.

Printed in the United States of America
Library of Congress Catalogue Card Number: 75-81701

SUNFLOWERS FOR TINA

Tina wanted to grow something. The back yard had a square of dirt that might have been a garden. Nothing grew because no one had planted anything. Behind the square of dirt was a board fence that had once been painted green, and behind that was an alley.

Overhead, the laundry flapped, and sometimes a cat walked the fence, and sometimes Tina's mother leaned out of a window to talk to a neighbor in another window.

Sometimes her brother Eddie drummed on the lid of the garbage can till Tina was ready to scream, and sometimes he didn't because the lid got too hot in summer. Then he and the other boys would turn on the fire hydrant and splash quickly through the cold torrent to cool off before the cops got there.

Tina asked her mother if they could have a garden.

Her mother said, "No. Where'd we have a garden? A garden's a luxury. We're not rich, you know."

"Out back," said Tina, "we could have a garden. There's dirt."

"You just try and grow something in New York City dirt," said Tina's mother.

R. SAM
CANDY
JACK & JILL
LOOK
CHILDREN'S WORLD
LIFE
SCHOOL MAGAZINE
50¢ a bunch

A block away, Mr. Samuels had his newsstand. He sold cigarettes and candy too, and sometimes he had a few bunches of flowers stuck in a pail of water.

Tina asked Mr. Samuels where he got his flowers.

"From a florist," he said. "I don't sell enough to get 'em from a wholesaler."

"Where do flowers grow?" Tina asked.

"Lord, I don't know. In the country somewheres. In a greenhouse, maybe."

"Don't any grow in New York?"

"I don't think so. I can't think where they would."

Tina had a nickel tied in a handkerchief.

"What will a nickel buy?"

"Lifesavers or gum. Most things are ten. 'Less you want to read the news."

"No."

"Lifesavers or gum then."

Tina bought cherry lifesavers. When she stuck her tongue out, she could see the lifesaver on it.

FRESH
MUSHROOMS
50¢
GRAPEFRUIT
3 for 40¢

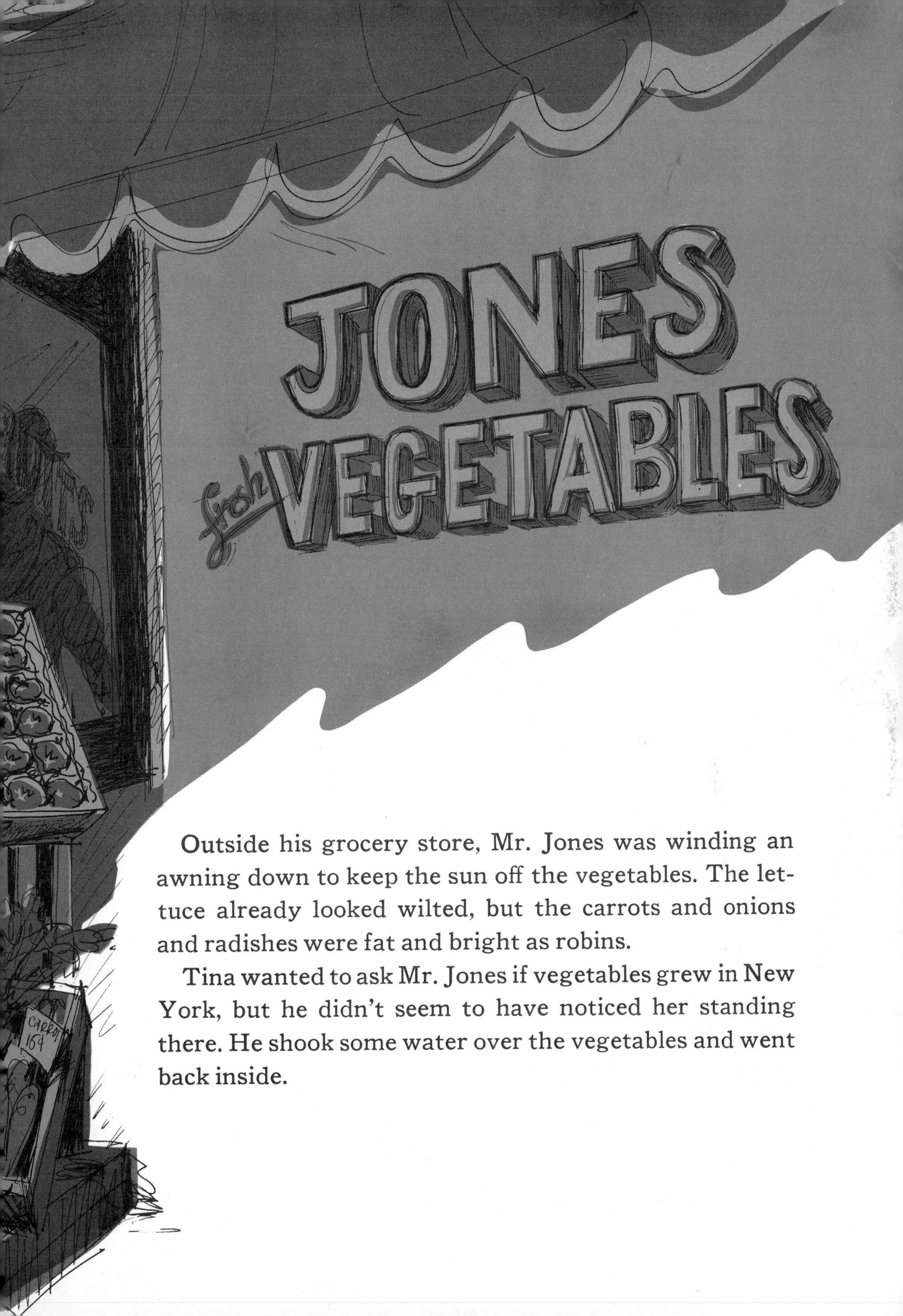

Outside his grocery store, Mr. Jones was winding an awning down to keep the sun off the vegetables. The lettuce already looked wilted, but the carrots and onions and radishes were fat and bright as robins.

Tina wanted to ask Mr. Jones if vegetables grew in New York, but he didn't seem to have noticed her standing there. He shook some water over the vegetables and went back inside.

The house sounded very quiet when Tina got home. Her mother was out at work. The upstairs kids weren't there. Eddie wasn't even banging around in the back room. Tina's grandmother sat in her corner of the bedroom, but she never made any noise. She was like a charred old stump, dark and gnarled and bent forever in the same position. Tina wished that she would only say something sometimes. Then Tina would be sure that her grandmother was really alive.

It was going to be a hot day. The kitchen smelled musty. The laundry strung between their building and the next one hung limply. Nothing moved.

Tina looked in the refrigerator. She drank a cool glass of milk and put the carton back on its shelf. It was then that she noticed the bunch of bulging carrots, with tops as fresh and ruffled as Tina's Easter dress. Lush and bounteous gardens sprang into her mind. Acres and acres of greenery grew before her very eyes.

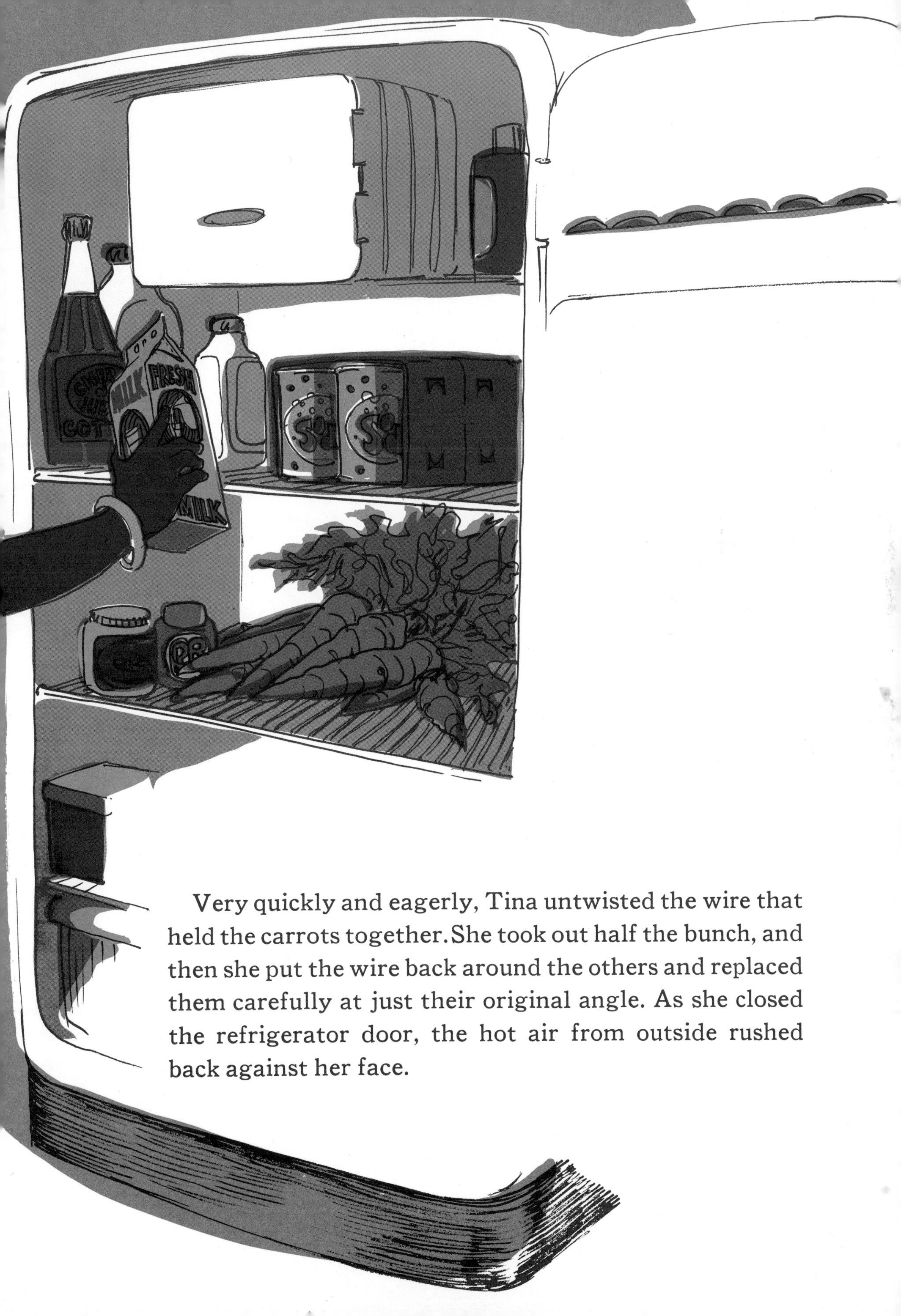

Very quickly and eagerly, Tina untwisted the wire that held the carrots together. She took out half the bunch, and then she put the wire back around the others and replaced them carefully at just their original angle. As she closed the refrigerator door, the hot air from outside rushed back against her face.

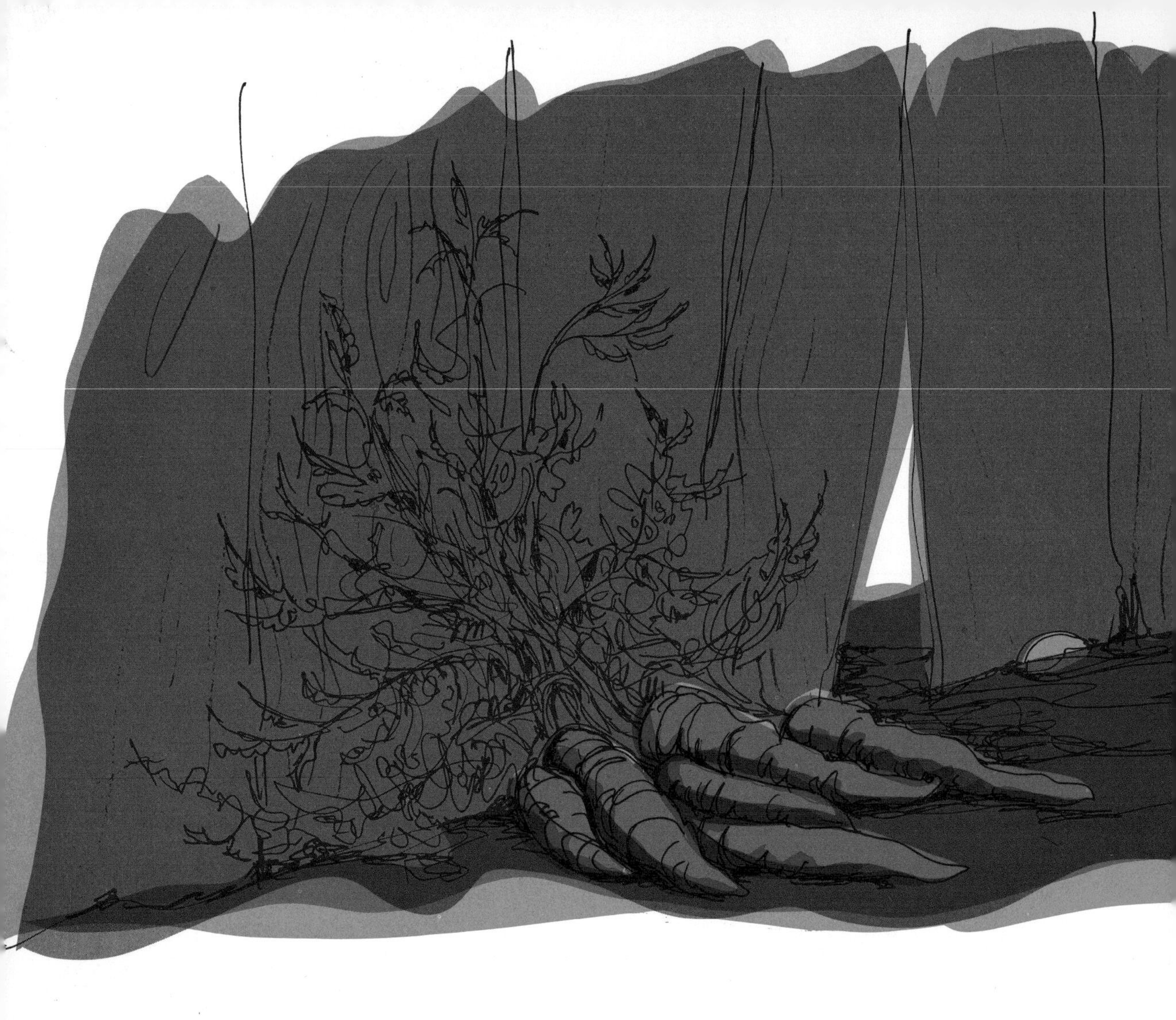

Tina took the carrots and a dirty spoon from the sink and went outside. She knelt down on the cracked concrete in front of the little square of earth by the fence, not even noticing that she scraped her knee. The ground was dry and hard. Tina dug at it with the spoon, but she couldn't make much of a hole. The handle of the spoon bent, and she hurt her hand trying to straighten it out.

Tina went inside for some water. The faucet wouldn't stop dripping after she had filled a glass; she gave up and let it drip. She poured the water into the ground where she had been digging and went back for more. The water made digging a little easier. Finally, she was able to bury a stubby carrot altogether.

At last, Tina had planted four carrots in a neat row in front of the fence. The green feathery tops stuck up cheerfully in the sun. She watered them with great and affectionate care.

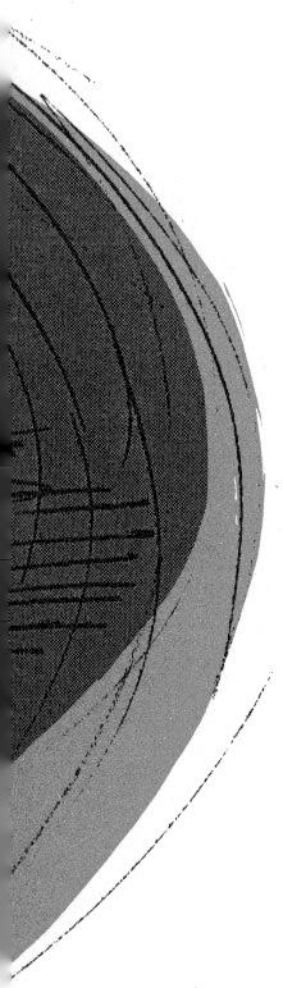

Tina rinsed the dirt off the spoon and left it in the sink where she had found it. She heard her grandmother moving clumsily in the bedroom, and went to the door. It took a moment for her eyes to get used to the dim light.

"Would you like a drink of water?" she asked her grandmother. It was all she could think of. She considered telling her about the garden, but it didn't seem worthwhile: her grandmother never answered her.

The old lady nodded silently, and Tina brought her a glass. Tina sat down on the floor at her feet. She dug the lifesavers out of her dress pocket, and peeled one off for her grandmother, whose hand shook a little as she took it.

Tina waited impatiently for her mother to come home. From time to time, she went out back and looked at her garden. The day dragged slowly on. The carrot tops began to droop in the hot sun.

From the next yard came the sound of Eddie practicing a tune on his harmonica. Tina hoped that he wouldn't see her garden before their mother did. She was sure Eddie would laugh.

Finally, the gate clicked, and Tina began sweeping the kitchen so that her mother wouldn't see her excitement. Tina's mother came heavily through the back door and began putting away a bag of groceries. Then she washed her hot face at the sink and changed into her slippers. "Phew," she said, wringing her hands. "Summer's here."

Tina danced in a circle around her broom. She did a low curtsy to her mother for fun.

"What's with you, child?"

"Oh nothing. Didn't you notice anything?"

Tina's mother looked all around the room. Then she looked at Tina with a puzzled expression. Tina laughed.

"Give up?"

"Give up."

"My garden!"

Tina swished past her mother and out the door before her mother had time to be surprised. She planted herself proudly in front of the little row of drooping carrot tops and spread out her arms happily toward the sun.

Tina's mother stood squarely in the doorway, her hands on her hips. She stared at Tina.

"What on earth . . .?"

"I planted it myself," said Tina proudly.

"You didn't — ! "

"Carrots," explained Tina. "They should grow." But her voice sounded uncertain by the end of the sentence.

"Oh no," said Tina's mother with a look of dismay. "Not our supper. You just dig those right up again!"

The summer went right on being hot and heavy. Even the pigeons looked hot. They waddled lazily around the flat rooftops. Tina's mother swore when they got the laundry dirty.

Eddie got a shoeshine kit from his uncle and spent most of his time hanging around downtown where business was better.

"Why can't you find something to do?" Eddie asked Tina. "Anything's better than just sitting around."

"Like what?"

"I don't know. Help Mom."

"I do."

"You don't."

When Tina started to cry, Eddie felt sorry and said, "Well, don't feel bad. Shinin' shoes ain't no fun either."

"I wish we had a garden." Tina said. She hadn't meant to tell Eddie, but it just came out.

"A garden?" Eddie repeated. "What for?"

"Just to look at. It'd be pretty."

Eddie sat down on the kitchen step. He put the garbage can between his knees and began to drum. He looked thoughtful. Then he said, "I'll be back," and swung through the rickety gate. She could hear him whistling as he loped down the alley.

Later, he came back and said, "I'll show you a garden, Sis," and he jerked his head toward the street.

Tina followed him some three blocks. She felt warmly happy.

Eddie stopped at the edge of an empty lot. "There," he said. "Sunflowers!"

Above them, the side wall of the first building bore the imprint of old walls and chimneys, as if a house had been turned inside out. Once there had been a building instead of the empty lot, and people had lived in it. Now, nothing was left except some broken bricks and crumbled mortar, and the black outline of rooms against the next wall.

Out of the rubble of brick and old cement, two stalks, taller than Tina herself, rose toward the sky. Each one lifted a yellow sun to light the day.

"How beautiful," said Tina. The harsh ruins of the broken building made them seem remarkable. It didn't matter that they weren't her own; they were there for anyone to see.

Eddie started forward to pick them for her.

"No, don't," Tina said.

He hesitated, trying for a moment to understand the expression on her face. Then he shrugged. She heard his penknife click shut inside his hand.

Tina was thinking of something quite different. She had suddenly remembered her old grandmother, hunched and silent in her dark corner, with only the whites of her eyes seeming to move. Her life was dark and old and crumbled, like the empty lot. Tina could only guess what it once had been. There didn't seem to be any sunflowers—any bright spots at all—left in her grandmother's life.

At home, Tina put on her yellow dress. It was almost too small for her, but the color was bright and beautiful against her dark skin.

Around the bedroom she danced. As she twirled, her full skirt filled with air and stood out from her waist, a golden disk of petals.

Tina could feel her grandmother's eyes follow her around the room questioningly.

"I'm a sunflower," Tina said.

Even though the room was very dark, Tina could see her grandmother's whole face crinkle into a smile. The whites of her eyes shone, and her thin shoulders shook under her shawl. Out of the cave between her cheeks came a distant rumble of laughter which Tina had never heard before.